PENNY

CURVY GIRLS CAN

SADIE KING

An off-limits office romance between an intern and the CEO.

Penny

All I've ever wanted is to design shoes, so landing an internship at a top footwear brand should be my dream come true. Instead, it's turning into a nightmare.

Someone's stolen my designs, my confidence is unraveling, and the devastatingly handsome CEO, Mr. Preston, is making it impossible to focus.

He's twice my age, completely off-limits, and yet, every look he gives me feels like fire. Can I salvage my career, protect my heart, and resist the man who's utterly forbidden?

Kyle

My company is bleeding money, and I should be focused on saving it. But then there's Penny—my young, talented intern with her brilliant ideas, irresistible curves, and delicate, tempting presence.

She's trouble wrapped in perfection, and the last thing I need. But keeping my distance is proving impossible…even if crossing the line could ruin us both.

Penny is part of the *Curvy Girls Can* series—short, steamy romances featuring strong, curvy women and the men who can't resist them. Always high heat, always sweet, and always happily ever after. Each book is a standalone and can be read in any order.

PENNY

CURVY GIRLS CAN

1

PENNY

I nudge open the door to the meeting room with my hip. The drink cart squeaks as I wheel it in, and half the eyes in the boardroom turn to me.

Janet gives me a withering stare, and I mouth an apology I don't feel. It's my job to bring the coffee in. I'm not sure how I'm meant to do that without interrupting the meeting.

I'm wearing my lucky green sandals today, so I give my toes a wiggle and keep going.

One of the account managers, Steve, is droning on as I wheel the cart to the side of the room. I take my time, carefully setting out the cups so they don't clink together.

By the time I'm done, all eyes are back to Steve. I

slink to the back of the room, but instead of going out the door, I slip into a spare seat.

Without needing to look, I already know Janet's eyes are on me, and I glance up to confirm it. She's staring daggers at me, and when I catch her eye, she ducks her head to the side, indicating the door and mouths, "Go."

I shake my head and her eyebrows pull down into a sharp V, meaning she's super pissed.

I bite my lip nervously, but don't leave.

Janet's my boss, and I've got no right to be at the design presentation meeting, but as an intern I'm supposed to be getting exposure to all aspects of the business. I'm not going to learn anything about shoe design if all I ever to do is make the coffee.

I sense another set of eyes on me and glance up. It's Mr. Preston, the CEO of the company. He's staring at me as intently as Janet is. But instead of cross, he looks curious.

My body tingles under his gaze and the heat spreads up my neck and into my cheeks. I duck my head so he doesn't see me blush. Whenever Mr. Preston is in the office, I turn from an ambitious design graduate into a tongue-tied girl who doesn't seem to have control over her body.

Even now, in the office boardroom as he stares

intently at me, the backs of my knees tingle and the hairs on my arms stand up.

I glance back at Janet, and she raises her hand in a shooing motion.

Mr. Preston clears his throat. "Is there a problem?" He's looking at directly at Janet.

"She doesn't need to be at this meeting, sir," she says, indicating me. "She's just an intern."

"I know who Penny is."

My stomach flutters when he says my name. I've got no idea how he knows who I am, but I can't help smiling. Which is a mistake because it makes Janet scowl even more.

"But she's supposed to be doing my expenses," she says, a note of desperation in her voice.

Mr. Preston must hear it too, because he folds his hands and looks at her curiously. "There's no reason why they can't wait."

Janet's mouth falls open. "But an intern in a design meeting . . . it's not really regular."

"Penny stays," he says in a voice that brokers no more argument. Janet's mouth snaps shut, and she looks down at her laptop.

"Now, I'm ready to see your designs, Janet."

She gets up slowly, and while she hooks up her laptop, it gives me a chance to gawk at Mr. Preston.

He's young for a CEO. He's got a young face, with a strong jawline and few creases. But the shock of silver that runs through either side of his dark hair could put him in his early forties, twenty years older than me, which means there's no way I should be getting all hot and tingly whenever he's around.

But there's something about his large frame and big hands, which he uses expressively, that makes me want to feel them all over me. I'm a big girl, but in his large hands I bet I'd feel tiny.

Janet starts her presentation by showing some of her best designs from past seasons. I watch her intently. There's a bead of sweat on her forehead, and she looks nervous. I wonder if she's always this nervous when presenting new designs.

I've got no idea what's in the presentation. She's kept her designs to herself, which is why I was so curious to be in the meeting.

I've been wanting to be a shoe designer ever since I realized it was a job. I love shoes. My wardrobe is overflowing with them: different styles, different colors, different brands.

I have a degree in fashion design, and when I applied for the internship at Sole Maker, I couldn't believe I got it. Sole Maker is the most prestigious footwear company on the West Coast. Their designs appear on catwalks all over the world, and there were over a hundred graduates who applied for the internship. I showed Janet some of my designs at the interview, and she hired me on the spot.

But I've been here six weeks and all I've done is make coffee and do photocopying. Half the time I'm stuck at my desk with nothing to do, so I sketch shoes.

Janet clicks the button and the next slide comes up. "Summer Collection."

I sit up in my seat.

"This summer we're going for comfort and color." She clicks through to the next slide.

It's a drawing of a sneaker. The drawing shows a slightly raised heel, and the light pink back quarter of the sneaker features silver stars.

My mouth drops open. It's my design. It's one of the designs I showed her in my interview.

"This is for the girl on the go who still wants to look pretty." She looks around the room, avoiding my eyes. "And the next one..."

She clicks to the next slide. It's another one of mine. A low heel with a pink lightning flash as a buckle.

"It's girlish femininity meets office wear. It's cute, it's got personality, and it's also functional."

There are smiles and nods around the room, but the bottom is falling out of my stomach. I only got the internship because she wanted to steal my designs. My jaw drops, leaving me utterly speechless.

Mr. Preston nods. "This is great, Janet." She beams, her nervousness turning to boldness. "Good work."

She goes through the rest of the designs, all of them mine. By the presentation ends, I'm furious.

But Mr. Preston is shaking her hand and telling her how excited he is about the new range. I should say something, but everyone here respects Janet. They'll never believe me.

I wonder what the women in the Maple Springs Businesswomen's Network would say. They're a group of successful women in my hometown and I got invited to one of their meetings before I moved here. I was too shy to say much and awed by the successful women around me. They'd tell me to speak up, but I just can't.

I slide down in my seat as everyone leaves the meeting. Janet walks past with a smile plastered on her face.

"Not a word to anyone," she says through her fake smile. "Or I'll have you fired, and you won't get another chance in this industry again."

She pushes past me, and I'm left seething in my chair. All I've ever wanted to do is design shoes and Janet has the power to take that away from me if I speak up.

I stand up, thinking the room's empty.

"What did you think?"

The voice makes me jump. Mr. Preston is the last person at the table. He's watching me intently with folded arms.

I swallow down my anger. It will do no good complaining to him. Who would he believe? The head designer who's been in the business for years or the new intern?

"They're great," I say carefully. "Really, um, original."

"Yes, original."

His eyes run down my body, and I sense each part flush right down to my toes. He seems to linger on my feet, and I'm glad I chose the strappy green sandals today.

"They're the same color as your eyes."

My eyebrows shoot up. "You're the first person who's ever noticed." Which shouldn't be a surprise. People buy a scarf to match their eye color, not shoes.

His gaze travels back to my face. "Pretty," he says,

nodding, and I don't know if he's talking about me or the shoes.

His gaze on me takes away some of the sting of Janet's betrayal. My heated body forgets what's happened with Janet and all I can think of is what it would feel like for Mr. Preston to unhook my sandals, slide them off my feet and slide his hands up my legs…

It's almost a relief when the door swings open and Steve bursts in. He speaks to Mr. Preston, ignoring me.

"I've got the factory on the line; do you want to be on the call?"

I slink out of the room, my knees tingling and my toes doing a happy dance in my sea green sandals. Yes, this was a good footwear day.

2
KYLE

It's the next evening, and my fingers drum on the desk as I stare at the screen. I frown at the numbers on the spreadsheet, but they don't change. We're losing money.

We've lost two big accounts, stores that no longer want to stock our shoes. They're too outdated is what they said.

We need something innovative, something new to turn the business around.

I pull up the file with the designs for the new range. They're good. Not Janet's usual style and I bet there's a story there, but if they win us some new business, then I don't care where she got the inspiration from.

I sit back in my chair and stretch. It's after six,

and the office is almost empty. There's only Penny, bent over her desk, probably working on something for Janet.

My eyes roam over the young intern. Her blonde hair is pulled back, and she's got an expression of concentration on her face. She's leaning forward, and I can see the outline of her breasts through her blouse.

She's curvy, with full breasts and a soft waist, the kind I can imagine sinking a hand into as I pull her toward me.

She's wearing a pleated skirt that goes all the way to her ankles. With her legs crossed, one foot hangs above the other, and her black sandal dangles from her toes. The office light catches the soft skin of her exposed arch.

I feel a twinge in my cock as I stare at those perfect feet. She jiggles her foot subconsciously, and the sandal bounces up and down. My dick hardens as I think about the soft skin of her arch riding over my cock.

From the moment she walked into the office in her one-off designer sandals, I've had a hard-on every time I look at her. She's been here six weeks, and I've only seen her wear the same shoe twice.

She's a woman who loves her footwear, and that's attractive to a guy like me.

But there's something else about her. Her sea-green eyes take everything in. She's smart and ballsy, as yesterday's meeting proved.

I make a decision; I'm going to put Penny on the team to present the new designs. I don't think Janet's giving her the opportunities she needs, but also because I want the chance to get close to her, to get to know her better. I already know I want her body. I'm eager to discover what else she has to offer.

I open the door to my office and stroll across the office floor. Penny's so engrossed in her work, she doesn't hear me until I'm standing right beside her.

"What are you working on?"

She looks up, startled, and her hand moves to cover the notebook on her desk. A blush creeps up her neck, which is endearing and maddening and makes my cock twitch.

"Uh, nothing, Mr. Preston."

She flips her sketch book over and stands up. It looks like she's sketching shoe designs, but if she doesn't want to show me, I won't press her.

"Call me Kyle."

She's blushing, and I want to believe it's because of

me, but it's more likely she's embarrassed because I've caught her sketching. She's adorably shy and I love that I make her blush. But if she wants to get on in this business, she needs to learn to stand up for herself. Presenting the new designs will help with that.

"We're presenting mockups of the new designs to our buyers in a few weeks. I want you to join the team in getting them ready and come with me to present."

Penny's eyes go wide. "Really? That would be great."

"Good."

Her enthusiasm and wide-eyed innocence makes me want to reach out and touch her. I want to run my hand through her silky hair and feel it tangle around my fingers. Instead, I put it on the back of the chair she's just jumped out of.

"It's a roadshow in Detroit. I want you to come."

Her mouth drops open. "To Detroit?"

"Yes. You'll need to book us flights and hotels."

"I'll be staying with you?" Her blush turns even deeper. "I mean, we won't be staying in the same room obviously."

I can't help grinning at her horrified expression. "I know what you mean."

She bites her lip, and it's so adorable that this

time I can't resist reaching out and sliding my arm around her waist.

She gasps at the touch but doesn't pull away. Her eyes are wide, and her lips are full. I smell candy on her breath and her floral perfume. She closes her eyes and parts her lips.

There's the bang of a door slamming, and we jump apart.

Janet strides into the office. "I forgot my coat."

Her expression is blank, nothing to show she saw us. Penny looks terrified, and I realize the risk I've put her in. If Janet saw us, it will be all over the office how Penny is sleeping with the boss to get ahead. I won't do that to her.

I won't let the needs of my dick ruin her reputation. I will not ruin the career of an inspiring junior designer.

I make a vow to myself that I won't sleep with Penny. No matter how tempting those soft curves and full lips. I'll treat her like any other employee in the office.

She's looking at me with disappointment, and I can see the desire in her eyes. Damn, it's going to be a hard vow to keep.

3

PENNY

My head's still spinning when I arrive at the office the next day. The memory of Mr. Preston's body pressed against me puts a bounce in my step, and I practically skip into the office in my bright orange heels.

I'm humming as I walk to my desk, and not even Janet's scowl knocks the grin off my face.

"What are you so happy about?" She narrows her eyes at me suspiciously.

I can't tell her it's because the hot Mr. Preston nearly kissed me.

"I'm coming to the roadshow," I tell her instead.

Her frown deepens. "I need you here at the office," she says.

Janet is my boss and her shoes used to win

awards. She's a respected member of the design community. But she also stole my designs without a second thought. I take a deep breath and straighten my back. "Kyle wants me to go"

"Kyle?" The muscle in her cheek twitches. "You mean Mr. Preston?"

A blush creeps up my neck at mention of his name. "He wants me to come to the roadshow."

Janet runs her eyes over me. "You need to be careful with him." She leans in conspiratorially. "He likes to flirt with the interns to get them into bed."

My heart sinks at her words. I thought there was a genuine attraction between us last night when he almost kissed me. But what do I really know about him, or any other man? A powerful man like that, of course that's all he wants.

"Just make sure you don't sleep with him. It's a small industry, and that kind of gossip gets around." her eyes blaze and a smirk crosses her face. "It could ruin a girl like you."

My cheeks are burning as I mumble a thanks. There's something sinister in Janet's warning and it's a reminder of how she could crush my career before it even gets started.

"I just thought I should warn you, Penny. You're just his type: young and naive."

She taps me reassuringly on the shoulder and flounces off to her desk.

I turn on my computer and slink into my seat.

As my computer warms up, I make a vow to myself. I will not be sucked in by the charms of Mr. Preston. I will not nearly kiss him again, and I certainly won't sleep with him.

4

KYLE

She's wearing platform sandals today with a ribbon that ties around her ankle. It's pinching the skin, and I'd like to take the ribbon in my teeth and undo it so I can slide her foot out of the shoe.

I shake my head and try to focus on my computer screen. But I find myself looking back at her, her soft ankle, and her silky thick leg.

It's been a long time since I met a woman I've wanted so much. Some men abuse the power they have as CEOs, but I never have. I've never slept with anyone at the office. I've never wanted to until now.

The door to the office opens, and a delivery man comes in with a bag of takeout.

Penny hurries to take it from him. "Dinner's here."

I stand up and pull open the door to my office. It's almost 7 p.m., and a few of the team are still here working to get everything ready for the roadshow next week.

Penny brings me my takeout carton.

"Eat in here with me," I say.

She grabs her food and joins me at the meeting table in my office. It's hardly a romantic dinner, but at least I get a chance to talk to her.

She's sitting just across from me, her breasts pushed right up against her cardigan, and my body's on fire. I draw my gaze away from her breasts to her face. "How are the roadshow plans coming?"

She finishes her mouthful of noodles, sucking the last one between her lips.

"Good." She nods. "I've got the flights and hotels booked. Did you want to hire a car or just use Uber?"

"Uber will be fine."

"Okay." She takes another mouthful of noodles, and I wonder if this is what she imagined she'd be doing when she graduated college.

"Why did you want to intern here?"

She finishes her mouthful before responding. "I've always loved shoes."

"You've got quite a collection."

A flush creeps into her neck. "You've noticed?"

I want to tell her I remember every shoe she's worn, how her feet look in each of them, and how they show off her legs, but I don't want to scare her. "I notice everyone's footwear," I say instead.

She looks a little disappointed, which gives me a spark of hope. Maybe she's interested in me too.

"Ever since I can remember I've been designing shoes." She chews her lip. "It's hard finding good shoes when you're a, um..." She looks down, embarrassed. "A bigger girl."

Her cheeks are red again and I want to take her hand, tell her she's got nothing to be embarrassed about. Hell, her curves are half her attraction. Instead, I tilt my head. "Go on."

"They need to be wider and sturdier, which are easy to find. But I like my shoes to be pretty as well. Feminine."

"Do you have any designs you could show me?"

The door bangs open and Janet bustles in with her takeout box. "Mind if I join you?"

Without waiting for an answer, she sits down at the table and stuffs some food in her mouth.

Penny looks down into her carton, making me wonder about the tension between them.

"I was just asking Penny if she could show me some of her designs."

Janet almost chokes on her fried rice. She shakes her head vigorously.

"They're quite amateurish, as you'd expect." She looks sharply at Penny, who's poking her chopsticks into her noodles.

"Nothing worth showing," she mumbles.

"What do you think of the presentation so far?" says Janet, changing the subject. "I'm wondering if we should start with the gold heel." She talks on about the presentation, but I'm not listening. I'm watching Penny. She hasn't taken her eyes off her noodle box. Suddenly, she gets up from the table.

"I need to get back to work."

I watch her leave the office, her hips swaying as she goes, wondering what it is she's hiding.

5

PENNY

I turn the sneaker over in my hand. The gold glitter trim glints in the hotel lights. I can't help the smile that spreads across my face.

We've spent the last two days presenting the new designs to potential buyers, but I still get a kick out of seeing one of my designs made into a real shoe.

My phone buzzes with an incoming message and it's Lizzie, a friend from Maple Springs. She's wondering why I haven't called in for the Businesswomen's Network meetings.

I ignore the message. I don't have the heart to tell her what's going on here. I'm too embarrassed that I'm in this situation. I can't tell those successful women what's happened.

"Another order has just come in." Mr. Preston plonks a bottle of champagne down on the table. "It's time to celebrate."

"I need to get these up to my room." I hastily cram the shoe back into its box.

"They can wait." He pours two glasses and hands me one.

"To the most successful roadshow we've ever had." He holds up his glass, and I clink it with mine before taking a sip. The bubbles tickle my lips as the sweet liquid fills my mouth.

"Shouldn't we wait for Janet?"

He shrugs. "I'd rather have a drink with you."

I almost choke on my champagne. After Janet's warning, I've kept my distance, but it's been hard. Every time I see Mr. Preston, my knees go tingly, and there's a tug in my core all the way down to my feet.

Despite what Janet said, I can't help being drawn to him. I want him to reach across the table and pull me to him like he did that night in the office two weeks ago.

I have another sip of champagne.

"So, Penny, when are you going to show me these designs you're always working on?"

The question catches me off guard. I take another

gulp from my glass and almost choke on the bubbles; champagne isn't made to be gulped.

"I don't know what you mean?"

His eyes bore into mine, and I can tell he knows I'm hiding something.

"You always have your sketch book with you. I assume you're not drawing the wildlife."

His eyes are twinkling, and I take another sip because damn, he's good-looking when he's being sardonic.

"More champagne please." I slam my half empty glass on the table, hoping the change of subject will distract him.

As he fills it up, my mind's racing. I want nothing more than to show him the sketches, show him it's my work.

But Janet swore she'd end my career before it's even started. And even if I was brave enough to go up against her, how can I justify letting it get so far? I let her take my designs and present them, and now I'd come across as petty and stupid if I said they were mine.

"If you want to be a designer, you need to get used to showing people your work." He sets the bottle down, and I take another big gulp. "You may want to slow down."

We're leaning on a round table, and he slides around so he's next to me. He's so close I can smell his cologne and the champagne on his lips. He takes the glass off me.

"If there's something troubling you, Penny, you can tell me. No judgment."

His eyes are serious now, his expression open. I open my mouth, but what can I say? Your star designer didn't really design the shoes, and now you'll appear ridiculous in front of all your buyers?

I shut my mouth again. "There's nothing troubling me, Mr. Preston."

"Kyle. You can call me Kyle, Penny."

He's so close now, and the champagne is fizzing in my head, and all I can focus on are those imploring eyes and those manly lips as he says my name.

Without thinking, I lean in and land my lips on his. For a moment, he's still. I taste champagne and his sweet sweat. Then his lips move, his hands move around me, and he's kissing me back. Firm and tender, and it's not just the champagne making my lips pop.

His hand goes around my waist and he pulls me to him, pressing his body against mine. I feel his erection through my skirt, and it sends a delightful shiver through my body all the way to my toes.

Then he's pulling away, his body moving away from mine.

"I'm sorry, Penny. I shouldn't have done that."

My face reddens. I'm just a naïve intern and he already regrets kissing me.

"It's not that I don't want you. I do, believe me. I want you more than I've wanted anyone. But it can't be like this. Not at work, not when you're the intern and I'm the boss."

"But how about all the other girls?" I blurt out, hating the way I sound like a petulant child. "You didn't mind kissing them."

He looks confused. "What other girls?"

But I'm already slinging my bag over my shoulder and grabbing the shoe boxes.

"I'm going back to my room." I turn and head for the elevators before he stops me.

I've just thrown myself at him, and he rejected me. If I could make myself disappear, I would.

I hear him calling after me, but I don't look back.

I get out of the elevator on my floor. The key to my

room is in my bag, and I have to put down the boxes and rummage through the front pocket to find it.

I'm about to put it in the lock when I hear the elevator open behind me. I glance back, hoping it's not Kyle. Instead, Janet walks out of the elevator. She's got a smug smile on her face.

"Enjoy your celebratory drink, did you?"

The way she says it sets off warning bells, and I don't answer. Instead, I push the key in the lock. It gets stuck, and I wiggle it.

She swaggers over toward me and pulls something out of her pocket.

"I just happened to be in the hotel bar. I saw something interesting." She holds up her phone. "Lucky I had my phone to take pictures."

I push open the door. I'm breathing hard now, my stomach clenching into knots. "I'm not sure what you saw, Janet."

I pull my bag and boxes into my room, but before I can close the door, she jams her foot in it.

"It's pretty obvious what was going on."

She holds up her phone, and there's a picture of me and Kyle kissing. She flicks through a few pictures showing us pressed together.

"Can you delete those please?" I say, although by

the way she's looking at me, I already know the answer.

"Oh, I don't think so. They're my insurance policy. That way you won't tell anyone about our little exchange of ideas."

I gape at her, the knot in my stomach turning to anger. "Exchange of ideas. Is that what you call it?"

She blinks at me, surprised that I'm talking back to her. But the champagne has made me bold.

"You stole my ideas, Janet. Stole them. That's a shitty thing to do to someone."

Her surprise turns into a thin smile, and she shrugs. "You don't have to like me, Penny, but you tell anyone about this and I'll show them these pictures. And your career will be over before it's even started."

My anger renders me speechless.

"Do you understand?" she asks. "Keep your mouth shut, and when your internship finishes I'll give you a glowing reference."

"You can take your glowing reference and you can shove it right up your..."

She slams the door shut before I can finish.

I slump against it and slide down onto the floor, tears stinging my eyes. This is officially the worst day of my life.

My designs were stolen, credit was given to someone else, I was rejected by the man I like, and to top it all off, I am now being blackmailed. I've messed up this internship and ruined my chances of being a shoe designer. Janet's right. My career is over before it's even started.

I grab my suitcase and start throwing clothes in as tears stream down my face.

6

KYLE

I wake up stiff and unrested. I spent the night thinking about Penny, her champagne-sweet lips on mine and her body pressed against me.

She ignited something in me I haven't felt in a long time. I want more than her body; I want to claim her as my woman.

It took all my willpower to push her away, but I won't claim her like this. Not on a work trip in a hotel like some sordid office fling. She deserves better than that. What I feel for her is more than an office fling. What I feel for her is real.

I tried to call her room, but she didn't answer. I need to tell her how I feel. Let her know how much I want her, that in the last few weeks I've developed feelings that go beyond anything I've ever felt before. That even though it sounds crazy, I'm in love with her.

I pack my bags and head down to the hotel lobby. We're checking out today, and I want to make sure I get some time alone with Penny before we go.

I hand my key over to the receptionist. "Has room 209 been down yet?"

She looks at her screen. "She checked out last night."

"Last night." I frown. Why would Penny check out last night? "Are you sure?"

She checks again and nods. "Checked out just after 6p.m." She pulls a package out from under the desk. "She left this for you."

"Thank you," I mumble as I move away from the desk. I take a seat on a lobby chair, and as I open the package, a note falls out.

Kyle,

You wanted to see my sketches, here they are. Don't think badly of me. I'm not cut out for the fashion world.

I gift these to you. Do with them what you will.

Penny

· · ·

Her sketchbook is dog-eared and some pages come away from the spine. It's being well used and well loved. I open it and carefully turn the pages.

There's a new design on each page. They're fun and feminine, and the style looks familiar.

As I flick through the pages, anger forms in my gut. It's obvious what's happened here. I knew Janet hadn't come up with those designs herself, but I didn't think she'd steal them from the intern.

"Want breakfast before we go?"

I look up to see Janet striding across the lobby and dragging her suitcase behind her.

My face must be thunderous, because she pauses. She glances down at the sketchbook, and I see fear flick across her face.

"You're fired," I say.

Her mouth gapes open. "I can explain..."

"How do you explain stealing someone else's designs?"

Her mouth opens and closes.

"I didn't think so." I stand up and slip the sketchbook into my bag. "HR will have someone pack up your things and send them to you. Don't come near my office again."

She regains her composure, and a cruel smile

spreads across her face. "I don't think you'll want to do that once you see what I have here."

She pulls out her phone and holds it out for me to see. It's a photo from the bar last night. A photo of me kissing Penny.

I try to snatch it, but she dances out of the way.

"I'm sure HR will have something to say about you moving in on an intern, exploiting her vulnerability and your position."

She's got a cruel smile on her face, and it's such a contrast to Penny's kindness that it sends me into a spin. If I wasn't certain about my feelings before, I am now.

"Is there something wrong with a man kissing his future wife?"

Her mouth drops open in surprise.

I laugh, because as soon as I say it, I know without a doubt it's what I want. It's what I've wanted since the day Penny walked into my office in those strappy green sandals that match her eyes.

I pick up my suitcase and walk past Janet who's still gaping at me.

Now I just have to convince Penny to say yes.

7

PENNY

I take the pile of sweaters out of my drawer and stack them in the big suitcase that's open on the bed. It's the next day, and I'm back in the small bedroom of my rented apartment. It's time to move back from Seattle to Maple Springs. I tried to make it in the big city and I failed. All I want now is the comforts of home and to be around my friends. I've got a bag of Fizzy Lizzie's bath bombs and I put them in the suitcase thinking about the hot bath I'll run later when I get back home.

I'm grabbing a pile of t-shirts when there's a knock at the door.

I pull it open and Kyle is standing there, suitcase in hand. I catch my breath at the sight of him. He has ruffled hair, as if he hasn't slept well, and dark stubble covers his chin. My stomach does a double flip then sinks. He's probably here to fire me for not speaking up when my designs were stolen, if he's even bothered to look at the sketchbook.

"I came straight from the airport," he says. "Can I come in?"

"You can come in, but I need to keep packing. My bus leaves in an hour." I open the door for him, and he follows me into the bedroom.

"You don't need to go, Penny." He pulls my sketchbook out of his bag and drops it onto the bed. "I fired Janet."

I stop midway between the drawer and the suitcase with a pile of t-shirts in my hands.

"You shouldn't have done that." The knot in my stomach is back. She'll ruin me now. My design career is definitely over.

"Because of the photos?"

I nod. He closes the distance between us and takes the t-shirts out of my hands and throws them on the bed. His hands go over mine, and the warmth travels through my body and starts to melt the knot in my stomach.

"I don't care about the photos, Penny. It's not a crime to kiss the person you love."

His eyes search mine as the words sink in. A surge of hope runs through me. Then I remember Janet's warning.

"But isn't this just another office fling for you?"

He looks confused. "What are you talking about?"

"Janet told me." I look down, embarrassed. "She told me about the other interns."

"What other interns? I've never been with anyone from the office. And I've never loved anyone the way I love you."

He looks so sincere, so hopeful that the knot in my stomach melts away, and I realize what I've been denying for the last two weeks.

"I love you too."

His lips crash into mine, and I kiss him back. It sends tingles through my body, and my heart beats double time.

He pulls away gently, keeping his hands in mine.

"I've loved you since the day you first walked into the office. This may seem sudden." He slides onto one knee, and at first I don't know what he's doing. Then realization kicks in and my heart races.

"Will you marry me?"

"Are you serious?" I cover my mouth with my hand and tears spring to my eyes. I can't believe this smart, charismatic man wants to be with me.

"Of course I'm serious Penny, you're smart and beautiful and you stir something in me. You make me feel young again, like anything's possible with you by my side. So please answer, will you marry me?"

"Yes! Yes!" The words are out before I even think about it, because I don't need to think. I know, deep down in my gut, that this is the man for me. And I don't need more time to prove it to myself.

Kyle's grinning from ear to ear. "I didn't have time to get a ring. We can go out and choose one today if you like?"

Tears sting my eyes. He gets up off his knees and kisses my eyelids.

"That's not all, Penny. I love your designs. I want you to head up a new division in the business. Shoes for plus size woman."

My head is spinning. "But I don't have the experience."

"You've got the creativity, the ambition, and the passion. We'll get a good team behind you, and you'll work closely with me. What do you say?"

"Yes! Yes again! Of course I'll marry you and get my dream job."

He laughs and lifts me up into the air.

"Hey, what are you doing?" I laugh.

"This time we're really celebrating."

He sits me down on the edge of the bed and pulls the suitcase onto the floor.

He kneels before me, and his hands travel down my thighs, down my shins, and to my feet. I'm wearing my house shoes with the green fluffy pom-poms, not the most flattering of footwear, but he slides them off reverently. His fingers run over my feet, and it sends shooting sparks throughout my body.

8

KYLE

I run my hand over Penny's soft feet, my fingers pressing into the delicate skin.

She's just made me the happiest man, agreeing to marry me and giving the business a new direction. Now it's time to claim my prize.

My fingers slide over the arch of her foot, and I lean forward and press my lips to it. Her foot quivers under my touch.

"Are you ticklish?"

"A little." She squirms, and I grip her foot tighter.

I kiss the arch of her foot and rub my bristles against her skin as my fingers knead the soft skin.

There are over 7,000 nerve endings in one foot, and I imagine the sensations that are shooting through her body.

My mouth travels over her ankle and up her creamy calf.

My cock is aching to run over her skin, and I ease it out of my pants. It's rock hard, and I run my hand up its shaft.

Penny leans up on her elbows, and her eyes go wide when she sees my cock. Looking straight at her, I run the tip of my cock over the arch of her foot. She brings the other foot to meet it and closes them together around my cock.

I groan as she tightens her grip. Her feet slide up and down my shaft, sending a shock of pleasure through my body.

Pre-cum shoots out of my dick, making it slick. She picks up the pace, and I groan as I watch my cock bobbing between her perfect feet.

It's erotic, but I want more. I want to pleasure her, and I want all of her.

I slide my hand up her leg, feeling it getting warm as I travel up her thighs until my fingertips skim her panties. She gasps as I touch the damp fabric.

"I want to pleasure you."

I slide her panties down her legs, taking her foot off my dick. My cock howls in protest, but I want to make her feel good before I take my pleasure.

My mouth kisses each of her toes before moving to her arches. I rub my bristles against the soft skin, tasting myself on them.

I kiss her ankles, tracing the faint veins with my tongue. As my hands slide up her thighs, my mouth kisses a soft trail from her ankles to her knees, to her full thighs.

She's breathing hard by the time my mouth closes around her pink folds. I kiss her pussy lips, licking and sucking, exploring her with my mouth. My tongue slips into her pussy and I'm filled with the taste of her, sweet and tangy.

As I lick her swollen lips, I slide a finger inside. She moans with pleasure, and I keep licking.

My tongue works her hard nub as I fuck her with my fingers. I've spread her leg apart, but she brings one foot around to rub against my cock. I groan into her pussy, and it spurs me on.

I lick her hard as her foot rubs my swollen cock. She cries out, and her pussy spasms around me. I press hard into her as the orgasm runs through her.

When she stops trembling, I sit back. Her eyes are dreamy and satisfied.

"That was amazing."

"I'm not done with you yet."

She raises her eyebrows at me. "How can I pleasure you?"

My dick twitches at the saucy look she's giving me. "Slide off the bed and turn around."

She does as instructed, and I kneel behind her and hitch up her skirt. My hand runs over her soft round ass. I position myself between her legs and slap my hard cock against her ass.

She leans forward, showing me her inviting pink entrance. I run the tip of my dick against her, sliding around her opening. When I slide the tip into her, she gasps.

"I need to tell you something," she says breathlessly. "I'm a virgin."

I'm poised at her slick entrance, and as she says the words, I almost lose it.

I swallow hard. "Oh, angel." My dick aches to push forward, push into her. "I'll take it slow."

"Will it hurt?"

"Maybe a little. Then it will feel good."

"Okay," she whimpers.

"I'm not using protection. I want to claim you and make you mine."

"Yes," she says. "Claim me as yours."

I slide my dick in a little more, and her pussy

closes around me in a vice-like grip, squeezing me to distraction.

She whimpers as I push in a little more.

"Touch yourself," I tell her.

Her hand reaches between her legs, and she moans as she finds her hard button. Her fingertips graze my balls, and I push forward until I feel my cock pressed against her virgin barrier.

"This may hurt, angel," I warn her before thrusting through.

She cries out as I push into her. Her pussy sucks me in, and shock waves shoot through my body. She's so tight and wet I won't be able to hold back much longer.

My hands grab her ass and I slide her up and down my shaft. Her fingers work her clit and tickle my balls as I pound her from behind.

My dick sinks in deeper each time I slam into her. With every thrust she cries out, high-pitched squeals that drive me crazy.

I sense her orgasm build, and as her body tenses I slam into her and explode. Cum shoots deep inside her as I release my pleasure. Her pussy grips my dick, and her hands cup my balls as I spasm against her.

We cry out together, joined in this moment, as I make her my woman.

When we're both still again, I slide slowly out of her. We climb onto the bed, and I hold her in my arms as she dozes.

My heart is light as I hold Penny in my arms. My future wife, my future business partner, my future everything.

EPILOGUE

PENNY

Six years later...

I can't help the grin on my face as I waddle out of the boardroom.

Kyle spots me from his office and raises an inquisitive eyebrow. "How did it go?"

"They loved it."

"Of course they did." He pulls me toward him for a kiss, and as his lips brush mine, I get the familiar tingle behind my knees. Even after six years, one kiss makes my knees quiver and my panties wet.

His hand slides around my pregnant belly and rubs the bump where our third child is growing.

"You need to sit down."

I wave him away. "I'm fine. I said I'd get the details straight over to them."

I waddle into my office, which is next to his, and sit down at my computer.

In the last six years, we've grown the business into a global brand. Our footwear is now sold in stores all around the world.

We usually travel together to meet our global clients. But since I'm eight months pregnant, I've been doing the meetings by video conference.

I teamed up with Stella from the Maple Springs Businesswomen's Network and paired my designs for plus sized women with her clothing brand. It's made us both very wealthy women. But my real abundance comes from my husband and family and the fullness of my life.

Kyle and I got married three months after we met in a small ceremony and had our first child a year later. Some may say that's fast, but when you're certain about something in life, you should just go for it.

"Someone else can send them what they need." He's leaning against the door frame, and the look in his eye tells me what he's thinking. "We're taking the afternoon off."

I check my watch. "We've got two hours before we need to pick up the kids."

"Two hours?" He laughs. "There's a lot I can do to you in two hours."

"Give me five minutes," I tell him. He saunters off and I try to focus on work for another five minutes, ignoring the tingle that's started between my legs.

I call the intern into my office and ask her to send the files for me.

"I was wondering, Mrs. Preston." She rubs her hands together nervously. "Would you mind taking a look at some of my sketches?"

She's fresh faced and keen and reminds me of myself a few years ago.

"I know you're really busy, and they're probably not good..." She trails off.

"I'll be the judge of that." I smile kindly at her. "I've got some time tomorrow morning. Bring them to my office first thing, and I'll take a look."

She smiles widely. "Thank you."

"No problem."

She practically skips out of the office, and I watch her go. I always make time for the interns, and I'm always on the lookout for new talent. Who knows, the sketches she shows me tomorrow might just be the start of a whole new product line.

But that's for tomorrow. Right now my man is waiting for me, and I've got two hours alone with him to look forward to.

GET YOUR FREE BOOK

Sign up to the Sadie King mailing list for a FREE book!

You'll be the first to hear about exclusive offers, bonus content and all the news from Sadie King.

Allie is a bonus book in the Curvy Girl Can series exclusive to my newsletter subscribers.

To claim your free book visit:
authorsadieking.com/bonus-scenes

Wild Heart Mountain

Military Heroes

Kobe brings together a group of military veterans who live on the side of Wild Heart Mountain. Can these wounded warriors find love or do their scars cut too deep?

Wild Riders MC

This group of ex-military bikers fall hard and fall fast when they encounter the curvy women who heal their hearts.

Knocked Up

A side story to the Wild Rider's MC. A secret baby romance featuring an ex-military demolition man who thinks he's not worthy of love.

Mountain Heroes

Steamy stories featuring the men and women from Wild Heart Mountain's Search and Rescue and Fire service.

Temptation

A damaged hero and a lost virgin in an explosive instalove retelling of the Hansel and Gretel story set in the woods of Wild Heart Mountain.

A Runaway Bride for Christmas

A snowstorm keeps this runaway bride trapped in the cabin of the mountain's biggest grump.

A Secret Baby for Christmas

Mr. Porter's Christmas takes a surprise turn when his daughter's best friend turns up with his baby.

Maple Springs

Small Town Sisters

Five curvy sister's inherit a dog hotel. But can they find love? Short and steamy instalove romance!

Candy's Café

A small-town cafe that's all heart. Meet the sister's who run it and the customer's who keep coming back.

All the Single Dads

These single dad hotties are fiercely protective and will do anything for the ones they love.

Men of Maple Mountain

These men are OTT possessive and will stop at nothing to claim the curvy innocent women they become obsessed with.

All the Scars we Cannot See

An instalove mountain man romance featuring a scarred ex-military recluse and a curvy girl on the run who steals his heart.

The Carter Family

Blue collar men find love with curvy girls in these quick read instalove romances.

Curvy Girls Can

Short, sweet and steamy instalove stories about sassy curvy women and the men who love them.

What the Fudge

A grumpy/sunshine Christmas romance.

Fudge and the Firefighter

A hot firefighter and curvy girl instalove Christmas romance.

The Seal's Obsession

A soft stalker, secret baby, military romance. Featuring an OTT obsessed alpha male and a sassy curvy girl.

Flirting With the Girl Dad

A single dad and curvy girl instalove romance.

Sunset Coast

Underground Crows MC

Short and steamy MC romance stories of obsessed men and curvy girls.

Sunset Security

A security firm run by ex-military men who become obsessed with their curvy girls.

His Christmas Obsession

A Christmas romance about an obsessed biker who rides

across the country in the snow to reach Cleo before he's even met her.

Men of the Sea

Super short and steamy tales from Temptation Bay of bad boys and curvy girls.

Love and Obsession

A bad boy trilogy featuring a thief, a henchman and an ex-military hitman who finds redemption with his curvy girl.

His Big Book Stack

The Underground Crows are called in to help an old friend do some digging when the woman he's obsessed with is threatened.

Kings County

Kings of Fire

Smoking hot tales of insta-love, featuring brave heroes and sassy heroines that will melt your heart.

King's Cops

Do you love police romance books? Then the King's Cops series is for you! Short, sweet and steamy tales of insta-love, featuring brave heroes and sassy heroines that will melt your heart.

For a full list of Sadie King's books check out her website

www.authorsadieking.com

ABOUT THE AUTHOR

Sadie King is a USA Today Best Selling Author of short instalove romance.

She lives in New Zealand with her ex-military husband and raucous young son.

When she's not writing she loves catching waves with her son, running along the beach, and drinking good wine, preferably with a book in hand.

authorsadieking.com

Thank you for reading my story! If you enjoyed it, please consider leaving a review, they mean so much to authors and it helps other readers find books they might like.

Thank you!
Sadie xx